Cat and Dog
The Super Snack

Cat and Dog wanted a snack.

Cat had a cup of raisins.
Dog had a cup of peanuts.

3

They poured in their cups,
and they mixed it all up.

4

It was better than before,
but they wanted something more.

They called Mouse.

Mouse came over with a cup of pretzels. 7

He poured in his cup,
and they mixed it all up.

It was better than before,
but they wanted something more.

They called Kitten.

Kitten came over with a cup of crackers.

She poured in her cup,
and they mixed it all up.

It was better than before,
but they wanted something more.

They called Pup.

13

14 **Pup came over with a cup of chocolate candies.**

He poured in his cup,
and they mixed it all up.

It was better than before,
and they didn't need any more.

15

Then, they all dipped in a cup,
and they split it all up.

It was better than before,
and they all got something more!

16